The Pied Piper of Hamelin

Retold and illustrated by Jane Ray

Collins

2

3

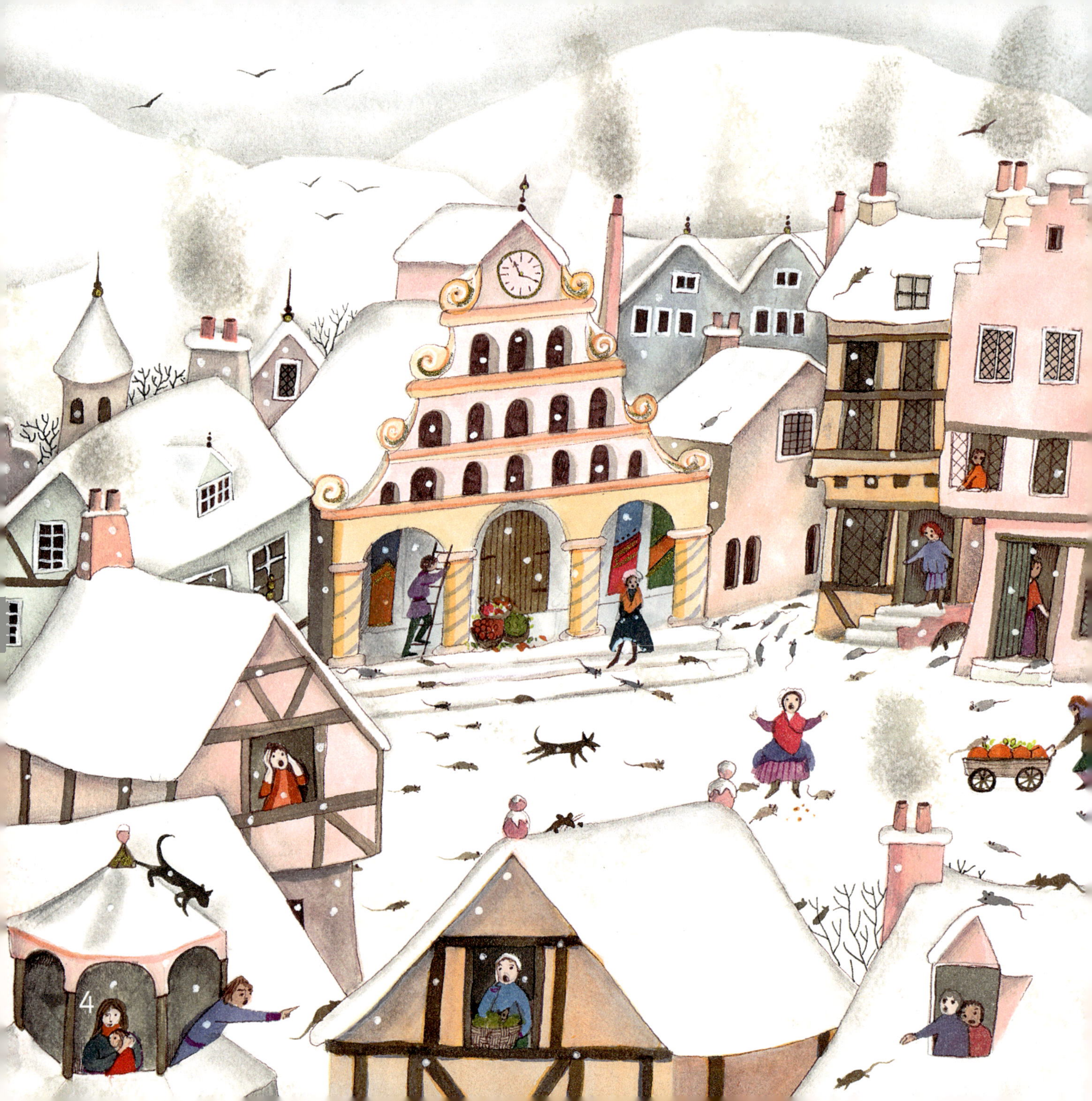

5

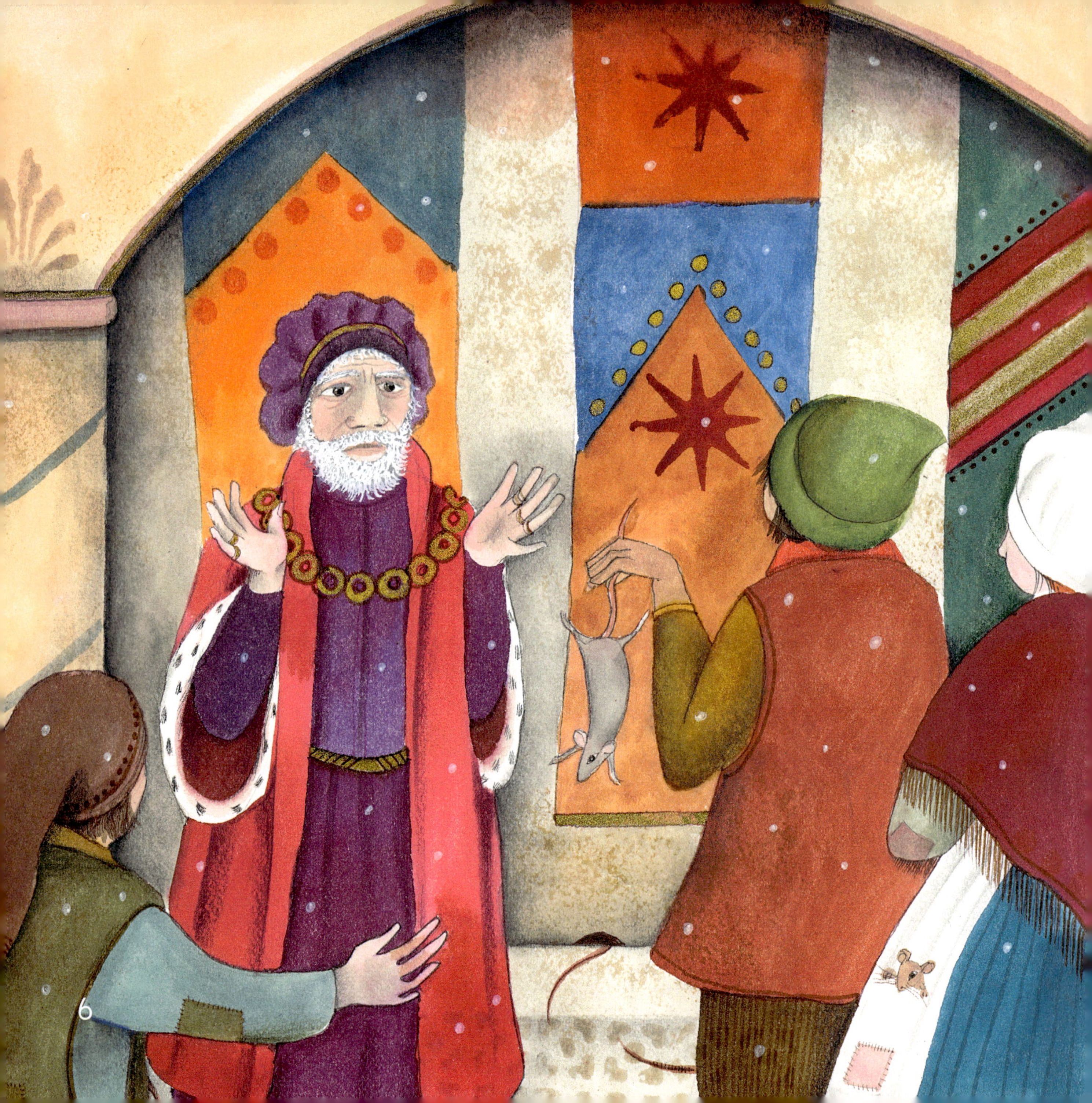

7

8

9

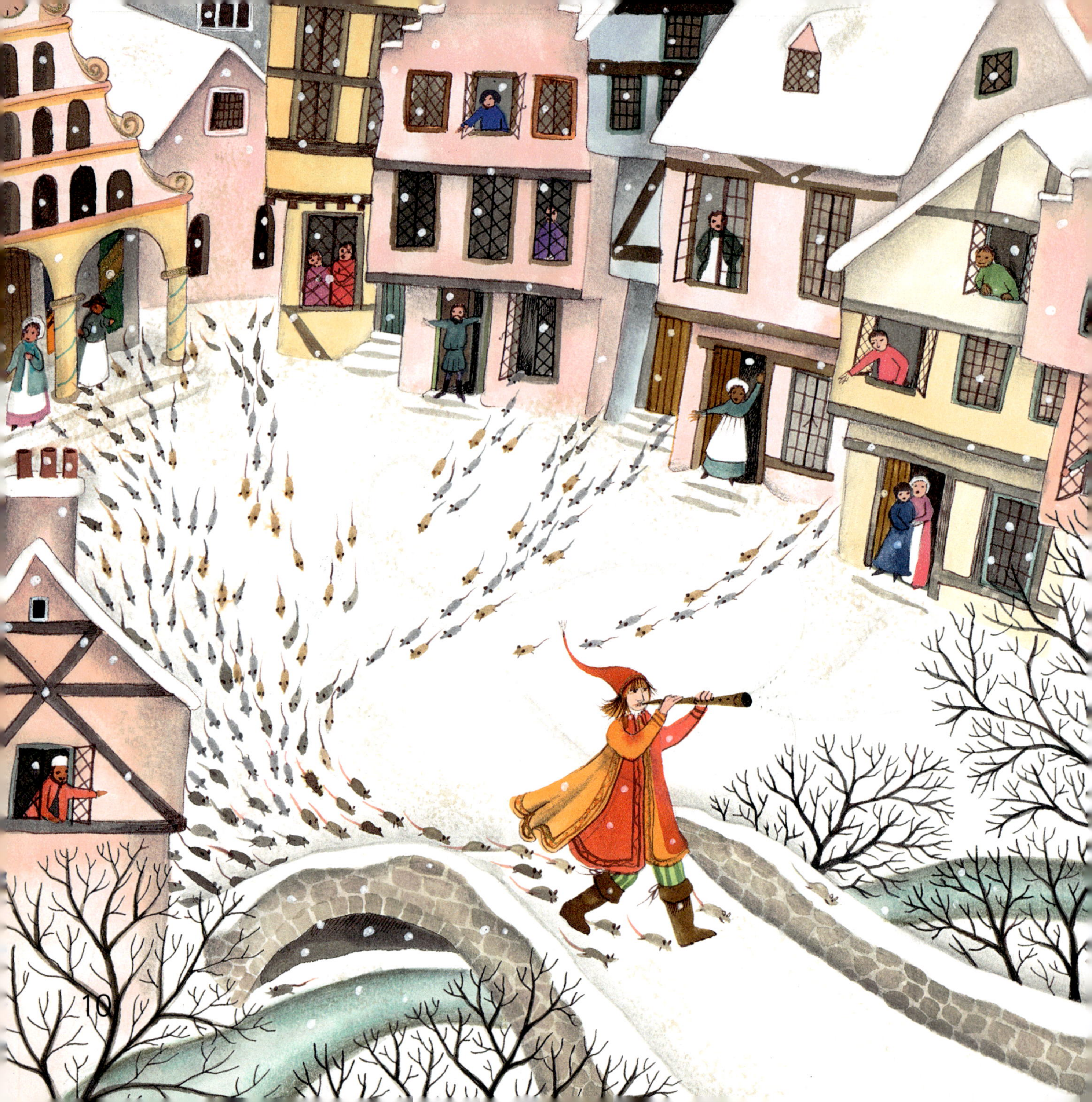

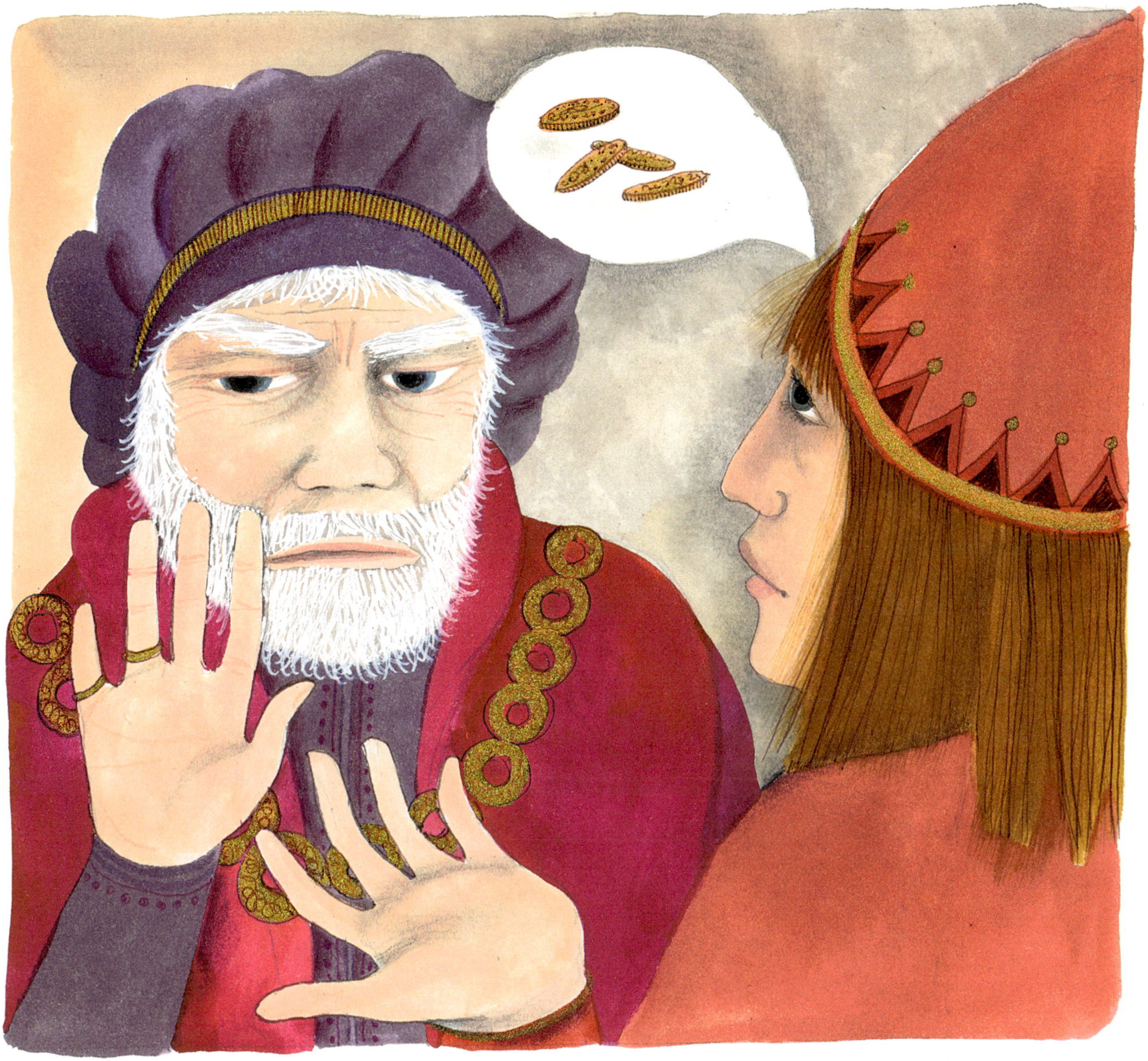

12

13

A story map

14

15

Ideas for reading

Written by Clare Dowdall, PhD
Lecturer and Primary Literacy Consultant

Learning objectives: use talk to organise, sequence and clarify thinking, ideas, feelings and events; use language to imagine and recreate roles and experiences; hear and say sounds in the order in which they occur; show an understanding of the elements of stories, such as main character, sequence of events, and openings; retell narratives in the correct sequence, drawing on the language patterns of stories

Curriculum links: Physical Development: Movement and space; Creative Development: Creating music and dance

High frequency words: the, of

Interest words: pied, piper, Hamelin, rats

Resources: picture of a rat, whiteboard

Getting started

- Ask children to share what they know about rats. Using a picture, discuss what a rat looks like. List words to describe a rat on a whiteboard.
- Look at the front and back covers of the book together. Read the title and the blurb, pointing to each word as you read.
- Looking at the front cover, invite volunteers to tell the group what may happen to the rats in this story.
- Look at the character of the Pied Piper. Ask children to describe him and his clothes. Ask children to predict whether he will be a good character or a bad character.

Reading and responding

- Explain that the children are going to be the authors of this story and make up the words for each picture.
- Look at pp2–3 with the children. Using traditional story language, model how to tell the story that is happening on pp2–3 using the pictures, e.g. *Once upon a time ...*